Translation by Arlette de Alba

Digital edition published by PI Kids in 2022.
This library edition published 2024.

Customer Service: 1-877-277-9441 or CustomerService@PhoenixInternational.com

Published by PI Kids, an imprint of Phoenix International Publications, Inc.

8501 West Higgins Road	34 Seymour Street	Heimhuder Straße 81
Chicago, Illinois 60631	London W1H 7JE	20148 Hamburg

PI Kids is a trademark of Phoenix International Publications, Inc., and is registered in the United States.

www.PIKidsMedia.com

Library of Congress Control Number: 2023949745

ISBN: 979-8-7654-0724-0

Bilingual Edition
Edición bilingüe

Rooster's Busy Day

Written by Erin Rose Grobarek
Illustrated by Angie Hodges and Pamela Seatter

pi kids®
An imprint of PHOENIX International Publications, Inc.
Chicago • London • New York • Hamburg • Mexico City • Sydney

Rooster starts his day
like most roosters do,
By calling out quite loudly:

cock-a-doodle-doo!

Rooster crows good morning
to his busy baby chicks.
Here come one, two, three.
There go four, five, six.

When Rooster feels hungry,
he pecks along the dirt.
He finds a worm for lunch,
and another for dessert!

Rooster finds a perch
high above the flock.
The hens strut slowly by
with a...

bawk,
bawk,
bawk!

Rooster's work is finished.
His busy day is done.
Now he dreams a dream
about the next day's sun.

You did it!
Now, read it in Spanish.

¡Bien hecho!
Ahora léelo en español.

El ajetreado día del gallo

Escrito por Erin Rose Grobarek

Ilustrado por Angie Hodges y Pamela Seatter

El gallo inicia el día cantando,
como hacen casi todos los gallos.
Con su clara voz dice feliz:

"¡Quí-qui-ri, quí-ri, quí!"

El gallo da los buenos días
mirando con gran emoción
a los seis tiernos pollitos
que salen del cascarón.

Entre la hierba va picoteando
y encuentra sin mucho esfuerzo
unos jugosos gusanos
que serán su rico almuerzo.

El gallo encuentra una percha
para mirar alrededor,
mientras las gallinas pasean
con un alegre:

¡Cloc,
cloc,
cloc!

El gallo termina su trabajo
y descansa en el gallinero.
Muy pronto estará soñando
con el sol que brilla en el cielo.

How do you say...?

The words below are listed in the order they appear in the book.

Rooster

Gallo

Day

Día

Cock-a-doodle-doo

Quiquiriquí

Chicks

Pollitos

Six

Seis

¿Cómo se dice...?

Las palabras se presentan aquí en el orden en que aparecen en el libro.

Lunch

Almuerzo

Perch

Percha

Hens

Gallinas

Work

Trabajo

Sun

Sol